Dedicated to the memory of:

Johnny French

SR

There was a town in Montana that never had a killing or anything like that in it until now. The police department there had a detective who didn't take nothing off of anyone. She was all business. Detective Jane Hartzman and she was born and raised in Montana. This town was her town. She wasn't married, but a fellow detective named Nathan Harding liked her a lot, he wanted to be partners with her except she was having none of it. Jane worked alone, now she had this case of a murdered girl that was found behind a dumpster that very morning. The girl was twenty years old, blonde, about five feet tall shot in the forehead, strangled, and raped. Jane's day wasn't about to get better either, she wanted evidence, DNA, fingerprints, everything. Jane got back to the office and got a phone call about another girl found near a ranch by some trees, she went out there and the coroner was next to the body, Detective Harding was there with the rancher who found her. Jane looked her over and told Harding that this was the same M.O as the other one, Jane thinks they have a serial killer on their hands and she knows this girl and her parents. The girl's name was Olivia Bates, twenty-one years old, brunette, five foot two inches. Jane found out the first girl's name was Sara Baker, Olivia and Sara went to college together in the next town and lived in this town. This was awful and she was going to nail this guy to her office door for this. No sooner had she gotten back to the P.D she got another call that a body had been found in the hills and she struck out for the hills, she was thinking it was a good thing she owned a jeep. Jane called Harding for the exact location and he told her where to go and he was on his way along with the coroner. They finally got there and the Sheriff was already on site and Jane did not like him at all, he had this know it all air about him and when he spotted her he was about to say something and the look she gave shut him up. The girl's purse was lying under her, and Jane eased it out and looked at her ID, it was a college ID just like the other two with the same MO. Shot, strangled, and raped, Jane was wondering what was going on here . This girl was from here and went to the same college, this guy had to be stopped and quick. She looked at the Sheriff and ask him,

"Who found the body?" He told her those two boys over there and she looked over at them, both were about nine or ten years old at least, she went over to them and they told her they were just out here riding bikes and there she was and went to call for help. Jane thanked them and told them to go home. Detective Harding told her something was not right here and why didn't the Sheriff have any deputies? That was very strange to him. She couldn't answer that one. Jane told the coroner, "You know what I want, so get going." He nodded his head and took off. She stood for a moment and was looking at the spot where the girl had been laying and spotted something shiny, it was the set out of a ring and it had crossbones on it. She put it in her pocket and walked back to her jeep. Harding walked up and ask her if something was wrong and she told him no and wanted to know if she could trust him and he said sure. She told him what she had found. Jane showed it to him and he said it looked like it might have come from a man's ring as big as it was. She ask him if he wanted to work these cases with her and he said, "yes, thought you would never ask." He followed her back to headquarters and they looked over the three cases together, they had Sara, Olivia, and Nan Gooden. All killed the same way that was a sure sign of a serial killer indeed. Then the phone rang, there was another dead girl in the hills not far from where the other was, Jane had to ask was there two young boys who found her and the answer was yes. This time Harding rode out with Jane in her jeep to the area and there she was, the two boys were sitting in the back of the Sheriff's car, he walked over to Jane and Harding and said, "I know what your thinking, this looks bad for those two, but they were up here practicing for a race over the weekend." Harding thanked him for clearing that up. He went over to Jane who was looking at the girl's ID that was just like the other three. It was from the college in the next town and her name was Julie Sims, a blonde, a brunette, a red head, and another blonde. It would seem the guy had particular tastes, same MO also. The coroner arrived and Jane told him to do his thing and get her the evidence. Not a boring day at least, just a sad one. She had to notify this girl's family now. The other three had been notified now to do this one, they had never had anything like this happen before why now? It would seem a lady killer had come to town and she wondered if he knew his set had come out of his ring? She looked at the Sheriff's ring, it was square top like the set and it had a set with an anchor on it. Harding didn't wear one, so she was still at a stand still so far, Jane had to find more evidence and DNA to fit somebody. She decided to go back to the office, but first to the jewelers to find special made for someone, it cost maybe a thousand dollars and it would have been in a gold ring. That was a start at least now to the coroners office for those DNA reports, when she walked in he handed them to her, all four of them, it was the same person that did it using the same gun, same rope, and all, it was a serial killer and they had to stop this guy. Even his DNA was the same in all four of them. Then the phone rang and it was another one by the roadside close to the hills where the last two were found. This girl had black hair and like the other four, she was in her twenties, college student, same college and killed the same way. The coroner looked at Jane and told her the girl's name from her ID was Betty Newly. All five of these girl's were from this town. This was getting stranger and weirder by the minute. The coroner said, "I will have the DNA report on your desk within the hour." She thanked him and just stood there deep in thought and Harding stood watching her expression change every few minutes. Then she spoke up, that guy lives here somewhere and knows these girls, we need to question the parents and find out who their friends are and who they dated. We need to get on it now. Harding agreed with her, so they set out to get started. Sara's parents told them none of her friends would have done such a thing, they were all nice and respectful and she had went out the only one boy at the college she attended and he was quiet and kind. Jane talked to Olivia's parents next and Olivia stayed pretty much to herself and her friend had moved away with her parents just before Olivia started college and they never knew of any boyfriend. Then it was Nan's parents turn to be questioned, they told Jane Nan had a lot of friends and they couldn't name all of them, but they gave her a nice list anyway, but they never knew anything about a boyfriend, so she went to Julie's parents, they couldn't tell her anything about any friends, but there was a boy she had been dating at school. They didn't know if they were still together or not, Betty's parents were more reserved because her father was the Mayor and she was an only child. So Olivia, Julie, and Betty's parents gave them a list of friends and two boyfriends and neither knew about the other it seemed. She told Harding about it and he told her he would talk with them and see what was going on with them. Harding went to talk with the two boys, but they said they hadn't seen her in two months because she was seeing someone else and both of them said the same thing. This did not sound right to Jane, something was off about it and she was getting to the bottom of it, so she decided that she and Harding would pay a visit to the college and ask a few questions there. They went to the school and ask around, it seemed the five girls were quite popular and hung out together, two were in a drama class and three were in music class together. Sara and Julie took drama and Olivia, Nan, and Betty played instruments and sang. Their teacher let them hear a recording of them and they were very good. Then a girl came up to them as they were leaving and told them about a guy all five girls were dating and neither knew about the other seeing him. She said he liked playing the field it seemed, then Jane spotted the guy wearing a familiar ring and stopped him to look at it and ask him about it. It was a club he belonged to he said, and when he walked away the girl told her it was a fraternity only guys belonged to and they thought they were it. The girl went on to her next class and Jane and Harding

were about to get in her jeep when
the girl came running back to her
and gave her a picture of the boy
the girls had dated and a water
bottle she said he had just thrown
away, Jane stood staring at her
and ask her why she was doing
this and she told her they were her
friends, the only ones she had and
now they were gone and she hated
that guy, because he used girls
and treated them like slaves to
him. The girl left then and Jane
and Harding took the bottle to
their P.D lab for DNA testing and
it matched, Jane looked the boy
up on the computer and found out
he belonged to that so-called club,

it showed him wearing the ring. She wondered if he had noticed the set was gone yet. If he has she reckoned he would be looking for it. Now all she wanted was him to come here and show himself, she wanted to catch him and she knew where he would go, right to the hills to do his dirty work. Jane had Harding go to his parents house and find out what he could there with a search warrant. Now they knew who he was Jake Blackly, the realtor's son. His parents were not going to be happy, he was twenty-two and tried to be a big shot, now she was onto him. Harding presented himself and four officers with a search warrant and began the search mainly in his room, they found the rope under the bed coiled up and the pistol in a drawer by the bed with a box of ammo, it was a forty-five just as the report said it was and they found all the clothes he had worn for all five murders he committed. The blood and everything on them, they had not been washed, just stuffed in a bag in the closet. Jake's parents were in shock and had no idea what he had done or anything, Harding told them do not warn him we want to catch him, Detective Jane Hartzman knows about where he will try it again and she wants him. Only this time he won't have the gun or rope, but he'll more than likely try something else. They were right of course, he went straight to the hills with a girl he already had tied up and pulled her out of the car, it was the girl that Jane had talked to and she was scared and crying. Jake told her they were going to have a little fun just like the other girls did. He threw her on the ground and was fixing to tear her clothes off and Jane stepped out with her gun drawn and told him, "He was under arrest for five murders and another attempted one." Jane told him, "you will be prosecuted severely for this and the others. You are going down, we have your gun and ballistics says it is the one, and the rope and your DNA, they all match." The officers stepped up and cuffed him and took him away. Jane untied the girl and Harding came up to make sure she was unharmed and told her they would see her home safely. Jane ask her, "why did he grab you?" The girl's nae was Alice, she told them, "He saw me when I grabbed the water bottle from the trash bin and ran to you and gave it to you." Harding knew instantly she was helping them. They took her home and went back to the office only to find Jake's parents there and they had his ring with the missing set. Jane got the set from her drawer and placed it in the ring and looked at Jake, he knew it was pointless to say anything and two of his club friends showed up and went to open their mouths and Jake told them to stop it was hopeless and pointless, because he did it, he killed those five girls and was going to kill Alice, they got him. Jane held up the ring without the set then produced the set and placed it in it and held up the gun and the rope and the DNA report and told the boys, he was done for, there would be no protesting unless they wanted to join him in his cell. They left and never said anything, Jake's parents apologized endlessly to all five girl's parents and told them they never knew their son was so evil or anything, because he never showed it. All those parents told them nobody could have known what their child would turn out to be like. Now there were five funerals to prepare and they were going to be on the same day, just as they appeared to happen, all in one day. It was really sad to think about and all the flowers and all the caskets were white and all the relatives and so many friends showed up and Nan, Olivia, and Betty's teacher came and brought the recording of them singing together and played it, a lot of people were surprised to hear it, most of all the parents of the three girls. Jane and Nathan Harding just stood by and listened, she thought it was great and looked over at their parents to see surprised faces. Jake's parents could not believe their son took the lives of those girls who could sing so beautiful and his father wanted to ask him that, but knew it was pointless. An officer came in and ask Jane and Harding could they step outside away from the others and the officer looked at them both and said, "Jake Blackly has hung himself in his cell, I just found him." Jane just stood there and told Harding to get in the jeep and the officer jumped in, too. They went in to the PD and straight to the cell, he was still hanging with some of the rope he had strangled the girls with, this was not suicide and Harding and the officer got him down and the coroner came over to get him and told Jane she would have her report immediately. Jane wanted to know who had the rope and took it in there. She had the officers and detectives come into the office for questioning. Jane and Harding both looked at each one of them in the face and she ask, "which one of you hung that boy?" "I want to know now." "I know one or two of you had a hand in it and when I find out your fired and jailed, I mean it." She knew he couldn't have done it himself and not with that rope, that was suppose to be locked up as evidence for those murders. The coroner brought the report to her himself and placed it in her hands. The boy was already dead before he was hanged. He had been poisoned then hanged, the only ones here were cops while everyone else was at the funerals. She looked up at Harding, the coroner, and the officer who ran over to tell her. Jane ask, "who all was here with Jake?" The young officer said, "Detective Jenkins and two patrolmen, Hood and Benning is all I saw here when I came in and went back and saw him, I was going to ask him about eating. I was in shock to see him like that and ran over to tell you." Jane thanked him and told him to gather those three men in here and now. The coroner sat down and so did Harding to wait, the DNA was being checked as to who handled the rope and when it was finished the technician brought it in to her and there were two on it besides Jake's. It was Hood and Detective Jenkins. Jane sat back in her chair and could not believe what she saw and read. The officer who called Billy, came in and said, "here is officer Hood and Benning, but I can't find Detective Jenkins." Jane knew instantly that he was responsible for this, now they would have to get a warrant for his arrest. Hood and Benning stood before her and Harding and Hood said, "It was Jenkins idea, I just helped with the rope, Jenkins gave him a shot of something and it killed him." Benning said, "I had nothing to do with it, I wasn't here when it happened, I walked in before Billy did." The lab report says it was a dran cleaner that killed him, Jane said. Hood would lose his job most likely for assisting Jenkins, now they had to find him. Officer Billy ran into Jane's office to tell her about Jenkins and where he went, he went out to the hills two hours ago. So now they had to go there, but why would he go there and why was he running. On the way out they ran into Jake's parents, they were coming to visit him, now they had to be told he was dead and how and why, but Jane didn't have the answer yet to the why. They told them and the coroner filled them in on everything else. Jane, Harding, and officer Billy went to the hills to find Detective Jenkins. They found him where Nan had been killed, Jane ask the big question, "why did you do it?" Jenkins said, "Nan was my niece, my sister's daughter and since her death my sister had to be hospitalized for it, that is why I couldn't take it anymore and poisoned and hung him. Hood only helped with the rope not killing him and he doesn't know anything about what I've told you." Jane and Harding took him in and wrote out his confession and he signed it. Jane took his badge and gun and Harding locked him up. They went to explain everything to Jake's parents as to why Jake died, it wasn't very nice either, because his parents went off angry. Understandable? Not really. Jane and Harding left Jake's parents and went back to the office and did all their paperwork and then went outside to Jane's jeep and Harding ask Jane if she would like to get some coffee and just talk.

Jane said ok, so they went for coffee and sat there talking about everything that happened the past few days. Then the Sheriff showed up and sat down for coffee and talked for a bit then he left them and they decided to get up and leave. Harding said goodnight and Jane went home to her pets. It had been a hectic day, but it was over now and everything is ok. So Jane went to sleep and dreamed good things.

ABOUT THE AUTHOR:

I grew up in a small town in Mississippi with my mom, dad, sister and brother. I've always

had a passion for writing. I use
to write poems and make up
stories all the time when I was
a little girl. I had one poem I
wrote get published in a book.
The older I got that passion got
smaller and smaller until one
day I quit writing and quit
making up poems. I guess it's
because I didn't have anything
interesting to write about. That
lasted a very long time. I didn't
even write in journals anymore
and I done that for years. The
only way I would write a story
or anything was in school. I

had to do book reports and essays. The day I first meet my husband it was light a spark lit inside of me. I felt happy. We have been married for almost six years now and it has been amazing. I recently told him and couple of months ago that I was going to write and publish books and he was supportive about it. I also have to mention my loving and supportive mother in this. She has been a big part of this as well. She helps me when I need it and supports me in everything I choose to do. I don't think I would have been able to this if it wasn't for them pushing and helping me through it. My brother and sister were happy about me doing this. They have copies of the other two books I published. I'm sure my dad would have supported me through this as well. I lost him in August of last year and it has been rough without him. Especially getting his phone calls. This book is specially written for him. He was a big fan of murder mysteries and had a nice collection of them. He was a major part of me writing this one. I'm sure if he was still here he would get a copy of one and have me sign it for him. I'm going to keep writing and publishing books for as long as I can. I don't write about just one thing, I have many stories to tell everyone about in different categories. Some may be love stories, horrors, or mysteries. Who knows what I will come up with next.